Remote Earth Short Stories

Volume 5
Moon Hab
&
Moon 3D

D.W. PATTERSON

Copyright © 2024 D.W. Patterson
All rights reserved.

First D2D Printing – October, 2024

Future Chron Publishing

Cover – Copyright © 2024 D.W. Patterson
Cover Image – Photo ID 221219811 © Elen33 | Dreamstime.com

No part of this book may be reproduced in any manner whatsoever without permission, except in the case of brief quotations for the purpose of review. This is a work of fiction. Names, characters, places and events are products of the author's imagination and should not be construed as real. Any resemblance to actual events and people, living or dead, is entirely coincidental.

Hard Science Fiction – Old School
Human Generated Content

Website: https://dwpatterson.com
Email: d.w.patterson.writer@gmail.com

To Sarah

TABLE OF CONTENTS

Moon Hab   Pg. 13

Moon 3D   Pg. 41

Moon Hab

"Is the surface of a planet the right place for an expanding technological civilization?"

- Gerard K. O'Neill

TO THE READER

In this story (and most of my stories) I know I am using the antiquated dating system, A.D. I blame this on the book Daybreak – 2250 A.D. by Andre Norton, which I read some time in elementary school (and of which I recently bought an old paperback copy). So, I was imprinted early with that dating system and think it sounds cooler than C.E. No social, political or any other kind of statement is meant.

Science and technology are important to me and I enjoy developing them as I develop a series. However, a problem arises if I have to reintroduce the science and technology in each story as the series progresses. For a reader that has been reading all along the reintroduction must be tedious and somewhat boring. For a reader entering later in the series (and I do like for the stories to stand alone) the lack of explanation could be off putting. So, as a compromise I have included the previous science and technology explanations in a Glossary at the end of this story, it also contains other facts about the series. Probably not a perfect solution, but the only one I could come up with at this time.

Chapter 1

2035 A.D.

Men had returned to the Moon only nine years before and now the first commercial settlement was starting, though it would be a pretty modest start, actually it would be just a single structure (and inflatable at that) but it would be home to several of the company's employees over the two week day of a lunar month.

Just south of Timaeus crater in Mare Frigoris the company had sited the settlement, *Tima*, named after the crater. Water in the permanent shadows of the crater's south wall would eventually support the new settlement. *Luna Limited* was one of a handful of companies that were racing to establish mining rights, manufacturing facilities, tourist destinations, and anything else that might bring in a dollar on the Moon. No one really knew what would be profitable but everyone felt that it was time to make a move.

I was above all the action, circling the Moon in the company's space station, part of the support network for those on the surface. I would be here for three months, that was a common rotation schedule, any more and the exposure to the normal radiation of space was considered too risky to one's health. Three months should be enough time to get the habitat setup and then someone else would take over the station.

I was here to take care of the work crew during the two-week long darkness at the job site. During that time they would rocket back to the space station where I would cook and maintain their quarters. Eventually, we would be able to "overnight" on the surface, but for now the cold of a lunar night was just too much for spacesuits and other work equipment to contend with.

Eventually the rotation schedule on the surface would be as

long as six months at a time, as the hab would provide more radiation protection than the space station. Long term plans would have most living quarters under three to six meters of regolith which would allow a permanent occupancy.

Site preparation had been done by the previous crew which I also worked with. The entire area had been blanketed with buried electrical cables through which a small current pulsated. The current generated a magnetic as well as electrical field which attracted the infamous lunar dust and kept it tamped down. Without the ever present dust floating about, machinery and spacesuits would function better and longer. The system was powered by solar arrays which had been landed and assembled previously during one of the lunar days. Eventually, the area would be cleaned by an electrostatic "vacuum" brought from Earth.

Delivery of the hab by *Space Trucks* Lunar Cargo Lander (LCL) was expected any time now. Already down on the surface was the current construction crew living in a leased rocket. They had worked a two-week day building up the site. In that time they had gotten the "Moon cement," made from an alkali binder and regolith, ready for rigidizing and anchoring the inflatable habitat coming from Earth. The US government had helped out, with sufficient compensation, by delivering water from their base at the south lunar pole. The company had also paid for the transport of the water by rocket to the building site.

The space station, along with other satellites, also provided a communication link to the ground. I was busy getting a time of arrival for the habitat when a call from the work foreman came in.

"Rogers, you got an ETA on the habitat?" he asked.

"Hold a moment Johns," I said.

I turned to the link with the incoming automated space truck. The LCL gave an estimate of twenty-two minutes which

I relayed down to Ralph Johns.

"Very well," he said. "I'm going to call a shift change then, a fresh crew will unload and do the preliminary on the habitat."

"Understood Johns," I said, and then signed off.

The ground teams work twelve hour shifts, one relaxing or sleeping in the rocket while the other works on the surface. I'm usually kept busy at shift change relaying information between the crews and the company. I had been at this for quite some time when I heard from the second crew leader, Joan Hartridge.

"Rogers, this is Hartridge."

"Yes Joan," I answered over the radio.

"Where's the space truck?" she asked.

I realized I had been distracted and had missed the scheduled arrival of the habitat.

"I don't know," I said, before thinking about how dumb that sounded, I was suppose to know, it was my job.

"Hold on a moment," I said.

I opened a channel to the space truck and queried its arrival time. The AI aboard assured me it had arrived and was awaiting unloading.

Okay, someone's hallucinating.

I called Joan.

"Joan the LCL informs me it has arrived and is awaiting unloading."

"What?" she said. "No way, we haven't seen the thing."

I knew the LCL was suppose to land on the other side of the hill from the job site so as to protect the site from any rocket blasted dust or debris during landing.

Could they have missed it?

"Okay Joan, hold on and let me run a trace"

Running a trace meant using the radio to triangulate on the space truck, wherever it was. I requested the LCL to fire up a location beacon. It didn't take long using the satellites to locate it. It was five miles from the designated landing area.

What the heck?

I called the AI aboard the space truck, it again assured me it had landed at the designated site. I was at a loss. How could the Em be so wrong? It was unheard of in my experience. I called Joan and explained what was happening.

"Jeremy, we are out here to unload and begin the installation of the hab, that is the only reason. You have six guys standing around under the porch waiting. Do you have any idea what that is costing the company? Someone is going to get their head chopped, you know?" said Joan.

"I know Joan, I'll get it figured out."

The "porch" Joan was talking about was the aluminum frame bucky-sphere covered with a sandwich of kevlar and high atomic-weight gel which provided some protection from the ever present particle rain and radiation of the lunar "atmosphere."

There were fourteen people on the surface costing the company six-figure salaries, not to mention my modest salary, and they were all standing around. I knew whose head would get "chopped."

Okay, calm down, what do I do know?

Then it occurred to me. I could have *Space Trucks* redirect the LCL to the site coordinates again and ask that the telemetry of the LCL be broadcast. I could then follow the path of the space truck, watching for any anomaly. At first the company refused to believe that the space truck could have landed that far away from the designated landing site. It took an hour before they got back to me and agreed to redirect the LCL with the telemetry broadcast available.

I would have to use the satellite network to follow the progress of the LCL because the space station was not in direct communication because of its orbital position. At the time the company had indicated I started receiving and decoding the telemetry. At first it appeared the LCL was flying directly toward the building site. I radioed Joan to keep a watch as the space truck would be flying over at a low level.

The LCL kept coming, its course was direct to the site. After a few minutes it flew directly over the building site without stopping. I radioed Joan.

"Did you see it Joan?" I asked.

"We saw something Rogers. It was going pretty fast."

"Very well, I'll call again when I see where it's going," I said.

I followed the telemetry information as it was plotted on my Emmie's screen. The space truck continued on its path for another five miles when its forward progress stopped and it descended to the Moon's surface.

It had gone almost as far from the building site as it had before. The telemetry stopped as the ship touched down. I called the LCL and asked for its status. It again reported being at the building site and waiting for unloading. I called the company, informing them that the same thing happened again. They agreed to send a team to bring the rocket to the job site manually, but that would take seventy-two to ninety-six hours, maybe more. I called Joan and explained what was happening.

"I think we need to get Ralph involved," said Joan.

It wasn't exactly what I wanted to hear but I didn't have any other ideas.

"Okay Joan, call me when you are ready."

It was a few minutes later when I got the call.

"Rogers," came the big booming voice of Ralph Johns over the radio, "what the hell is going on?"

"I'm not sure Ralph," I said. "The AI in the space truck seems to be in some kind of denial, it keeps telling me it is in position and ready to unload. I've informed the company and they are sending some people to bring the ship in manually."

"When?" he asked.

"Seventy-two to ninety-six hours they said."

"What? We're suppose to sit on our butts for three to four days? Do you know how much money that is costing the company? Not to mention the mess it will make to the schedule," he said.

"I understand Ralph, but what else can we do?" I asked.

"We can go get it," he said. "How far away is the damn thing?"

"It's approximately five miles east of the building site," I said.

"Okay," he said, "you stay on Space Truck's back, try to get them here sooner. I'm going to take some men and the hauler and find that rocket."

"Be careful Ralph," I said.

"Yeah," he said and the call was dropped.

Chapter 2

The expedition to the space truck had been gone about twelve hours when I got a call from Joan.

"Rogers, we've lost contact with Ralph and the others. Can you try to raise him?"

"Okay Joan, give me a minute," I said.

I tried, through the satellite network, to get Ralph on the radio but failed.

"Can't raise him Joan," I said to Hartridge. "I should be near enough to the area on the next orbit pass to try again."

Besides the radio, I readied a telescope that I thought might be powerful enough to see something on the surface. I assigned an Em to operate the scope and to alert me of any sighting. It would be another twenty minutes before the station would be over the landing site of the space truck.

I followed the station's ground track and as it closed on the area I queried the Em operating the telescope. At first it reported nothing, then it reported identifying the LCL on the Moon's surface. Then I urged it to scan the area to the west of the landing site. I waited a couple of minutes, the Em reported finding something. Eventually, a picture appeared on my Emmie's screen. As I zoomed in I thought I could make out the hauler that Johns would have used to bring back the hab. There wasn't enough resolution to make out any spacesuited figures.

I called Hartridge.

"Joan, the telescope on board has found the rocket and the hauler, there's not enough resolution to see any of the crew. It appears that the hauler has crashed, I say this because it is resting at an awkward angle in the image. I estimate they made it within a mile of the rocket."

"Okay Rogers, I plan on sending out a search party," she said.

"But you don't have a transport," I said.

"They'll go out on foot, the suit radios should work if they get within a mile of the hauler," she said.

"I should get the company's approval," I said. "We should have called them before Ralph went out."

"Well, Ralph wasn't going to wait for approval and I'm not either. You do what you think is right."

"Very well Joan, goodbye," I said.

The hauler wrecked, four crew missing including the lead foreman, and now another group was going. I didn't know if I wanted to inform the company or not, but it was my job.

"Rogers," said the head of operations after the communications delay. "You are being paid to keep us informed and now you tell me this has been going on for hours."

"I'm sorry Mr. Dravers but if you know Ralph Johns, you know he's not one to wait for permission."

"Still, you could have informed us immediately after you found out. I'm afraid this delay is unacceptable. I don't imagine you will be offered another contract with the company."

"Very well, Mr. Dravers, but what does the company want me to do now?"

"We are informing Joan Hartridge that she is now lead foreman of the job site. She will dismiss Ralph Johns from his duties when he returns. Mr. Johns will be flown out as soon as possible. We are moving up the replacement crew and sending a new hauler in case the present one is damaged as you expect. They should be there by next week if we can arrange the flight. I will let you know when I have confirmed.

"And finally, we are sending your replacement with the crew, you will return to Earth with Mr. Johns. That is all."

The communication was terminated, I was terminated, but at least I had another week. I needed to contact Joan on the surface and let her know.

"They're back Rogers," said Joan before I could tell her what had transpired on the company call. "Ralph's dead but the other three of them are okay, although one is injured."

"Who?" I asked.

"George, apparently he was thrown from the hauler when it went in the crater. We're trying to figure out how badly he is injured right now. They were also able to carry Ralph's body."

"Okay, I'll relay to the company, you may get a call from them soon, in which case you can tell them."

"Call coming in now Rogers, I'll get back to you," said Joan.

Later Joan called again.

"That's right Rogers, the company wants you down here right now to replace George," said Joan.

"But I'm not trained for surface operations," I said.

"Doesn't make a difference apparently. Instead of going back to Earth with Ralph's body, you'll support the surface operations when the new crew gets here and we get back on schedule."

"Okay Joan, bye."

As I was sitting there a communication came through telling me what Joan had already told me. I noticed Dravers didn't tell me personally.

Okay, the good news is I can finish out my contract and get paid. The bad news is I don't want to.

But I stayed, and the following week I was on the Lunar Personnel Lander (LPL), which was very much like the LCL only outfitted for people. Both types of landers consisted of two cylinders with rockets for maneuvering and take-off and landing. The cylinders were joined by scaffold. Think beer cans with rockets. In addition, the LCL had a large cargo container attached to the underside of the scaffolding.

With the rest of the new crew heading for the surface of the Moon. I had turned over my duties to the new station monitor, Elizabeth.

The LPL deposited us behind the hill that served as a blast shield for the job site. Without the hauler, which was still abandoned four miles away, we would have to "walk" the rest of the way. I had a little training for walking in one-sixth Earth gravity but not enough to keep up with the rest of the crew. By the time we rounded the base of the hill and could see the job site, the slowest member of the new crew was under the porch and the old crew was heading out, towards me. I expected I was a source of derisive comments even if I couldn't hear the personal channels being used to make those comments.

As I neared the job site I felt a sensation on my skin that was difficult to place but not bothersome. I dismissed it and continued my awkward stride, eventually reaching the porch with the rest of the crew. It was then that Joan gave her talk.

"Now, that we are all here," she said. "I want to talk to you about what to expect during your three month stay.

"We are now a week behind schedule and we still do not have the habitat. Space Trucks has assured us that they will deliver the hab by the end of this week, that is in two days. Unfortunately, that will only leave us two days to unload and move the hab into place before the beginning of the two week night. So that is our immediate goal.

"At that point we will all, except for Rogers, leave on the LPL for the station. It has been decided that Rogers will stay here and keep the rocket at a higher level of readiness than usual during the night-over. This means that we can come back to the job site and be ready to resume our duties immediately instead of the usual startup time required after a shutdown.

"Rogers you will call the company after this meeting is over for a description of your new duties."

I was a bit stunned. As far as I knew no one had ever overnighted on the Moon. In the space station I had passed in and out of sunlight over and over during an orbit. I had never experienced a two-week night, no one had ever experienced a two-week night on the Moon, or on Earth. I definitely needed to make a call. I headed for the rocket, even before Joan had finished the rest of her briefing.

It was possible from the surface of the Moon, at the job site location, to contact Earth at any time except for a few short blackouts that occurred because of communication satellite availability. In the rocket, ready to call, I found we were in one of those blackout periods. It would be over in fifteen minutes. I had time to think.

Ridiculous. How am I suppose to do this? They want me to be the first person ever to overnight on the Moon? Crazy. Dravers must be crazy. I don't have to do it. I won't do it. They can't make me do it. I wonder if the LPL has left? I'll get on board and head back to the station. I'll go home with Ralph's body. Who do they think they are dealing with? I'm not an idiot.

Or maybe I was, anyway a call was coming in.

"Job site, this is Rogers," I said.

"Rogers, good, this is Dravers. I want to talk to you. I suppose that Joan has told you what we want you to do?"

"Yeah, she told me," I said. "But I'm not sure I want to do it."

"But Rogers, we've got to do everything we can to get this project back on schedule. You are the perfect person to help us with that."

I was surprised that I was the perfect person.

"Why am I the perfect person?" I asked.

"Because with your experience aboard the station, you have all the necessary skills to keep the job site going during the two week night. You've done it aboard the station for as long as that, all alone," he said.

I realized he was right. I had done most of the chores aboard the station that I would need to do to keep the job site going, and I had been alone for almost two weeks. But Dravers had just threatened me with dismissal a short time ago. Why should I do this for the company?

"I was headed for Earth not long ago, by company decree, if you remember. And now I'm to stay here in a totally different capacity for the good of the company?"

"Rogers, I know I was a little hasty, but getting this hab built on schedule could make or break the company. You will be well rewarded for going above and beyond, I can assure you. I am sorry for what occurred before but I and the whole company, that includes many of those you have worked with or are currently working with. It means their jobs also. So I'm asking you to forgive my rashness and do this for the company and the employees."

My righteous indignation subsided, the man was making an effort to atone, unfortunately, I probably would have to do it. I was always a sucker for an apology.

"Okay Rick, I'll do it," I heard myself say, though not wanting to hear myself say it.

"Great Rogers, me and the company owe you."

The call over, I sat for a moment thinking that I had made a good decision. Then I thought about being alone on the surface of the Moon for two weeks, in the dark, and I wanted to run away, but the others were beginning to come through the airlock.

Chapter 3

The Space Trucks company finally came through. They manually flew their rocket and landed it at the job site, that is on the other side of the hill. I had a chance to talk with the Space Trucks pilot while she was waiting for the hab to be unloaded. We sat down in the rocket's dining room over a cup of coffee.

"I'm Jeremy Rogers," I said, as I poured her a cup of coffee.

"Jen Blalock," she said.

"Ms. Blalock, I was wondering, I use to be the monitor on the company's space station and I was responsible for getting Space Trucks and you out here. I was just wondering, do you have any idea why the AI couldn't land the LCL at the job site? I mean, did you have any problem?"

"Well, Mr. Rogers, I don't know why the AI had such a problem, but I brought the rocket in manually, so there were many automated systems that didn't come into play."

"Like a sensor?" I asked.

"Maybe," she said. "Why did you say that?"

"Oh, just something that occurred to me as I was walking from the landing area to the porch the other day."

"You don't have a hauler?" she asked.

"No, ours is out of commission," I said.

"Well, how are you going to get the hab around the hill?"

"I don't know," I said. "Joan's got a plan. She's the lead foreman on the job."

"I see," she said, but I knew she didn't, because I had no idea what Joan was doing either.

It was afternoon before I saw how the crew was moving the hab. As they came around the foot of the hill I could see they were carrying it on a frame. Two crew members in front, two behind, and two on each side. This was not as silly as it sounds because although the inflatable hab might weigh over a ton on Earth, here on the Moon, it was less than four-hundred pounds. So eight crew could handle it if careful. And they were being careful, with Joan walking in front and calling out the choreographed operation. Another few hours and they had the hab in position and they quit for the "day."

The next day, except for a few finishing touches, the new crew and old crew packed for the trip to the space station and a trip home for George and what was left of Ralph. Some had already started for the LPL, Joan stopped to see me.

"Well Rogers, you are about to make history," she said.

"You mean over-nighting?" I said.

"Yeah, no one's ever done it before on the Moon. Those guys at the poles have almost continuous sunlight, except when they're working down in one of the craters. But that's just shift work. So you will have the record soon."

"I'll have it alright," I said. "I hope that I'll want it."

"Nervous?" she asked.

"Yeah, not so much staying here alone," I said. "But if something happens I'm stuck here."

"You're sitting in a rocket Rogers."

"I know, but I don't know how to fly it and apparently an AI has trouble flying into the area so why should one be able to fly out?"

"I see," she said, as if she had just realized what I was saying.

"Well, the LPL can come back, that's a human pilot," she said.

"Yeah, but a night landing," I said.

She paused.

"Nothing's going to go wrong Rogers, we'll be back before you know it," she said as she turned to process through the airlock.

And in a couple of minutes I was alone.

There is nothing like being alone in a place that was just full of people to make one hyper-sensitive. Outside the sun was just passing below the horizon and without any atmosphere to scatter the light it was just like the turning out of a light bulb. It was dark outside, as dark as I've ever seen, the only consolation was the emergent stars which I had also noticed from the space station.

But as the temperature dropped there were sounds, sounds such as I had not heard before aboard a rocketship. Besides the metal stress, there were the different tanks of liquid and gases, the cycling of heaters and pumps, and the ramp up and down of the environmental system.

I felt suddenly cold, whether the chill was from a temperature change or the quiet darkness. I sat for another few minutes in the control room listening to these sounds before deciding that the first thing I would do during my command of the rocket was to take a rest in my bunk.

By turning on the small fan in my cabin I was able to drown out most of the sounds of the rocket and after some minutes I fell asleep. I must have slept for a while when I woke suddenly.

That's it. It must be the electrical grid.

I had awoken with the thought that the electric grid used to attract the Moon's dust and keep it tamped down might cause a problem with some sensor necessary for the AI aboard a rocket to land in the area of the job site. The electrical and magnetic fields were confusing the AI somehow. I wasn't an engineer so I didn't know how, but I would pass along my thoughts to those who might know. Anyhow, it calmed my mind enough to get finish a nights sleep.

When I woke I wrote up my idea and sent it to the company, then I started my assignments. Mostly, I went around checking the equipment which wasn't necessary since it was all monitored from the control room, but the company had decided that since this was a first, it would be advisable to make a personal inspection. I would do my inspections twice during a twenty-four hour period.

It was sometime after the middle of the two-week night, during which I had started looking forward to my inspection rounds, I was counting them down to the end of my stay. Then, down in environmental, I heard a strange sound.

Removing several access panels I finally found the noise, the pump in the circuit responsible for scrubbing the carbon dioxide was making the racket, it also felt warm to the touch. The system was regenerative in that it used multiple beds of amine beads which removed the carbon dioxide from the air the fans caused to circulate across the beds. As they removed the carbon dioxide the beads got quite hot, the pump and coolant kept them from getting too hot. Once saturated, those beds were exposed to the vacuum to out gas while other active beds took there place.

Without the pump the beads would heat up and crack and fail quickly. Carbon dioxide would then build up to dangerous levels. I had learned during my training for manning the space station that carbon dioxide poisoning could cause cardiac problems as well as impaired judgment. At higher levels it could cause convulsions, coma and even death.

I would have to replace the pump before carbon dioxide levels became too high. I headed for the machine locker to get the correct replacement. But no matter how many times I went through the inventory there wasn't a pump like it. I wondered?

The answer was found in the maintenance logs. Apparently, that pump had failed before and been replaced by the spare. But that spare had never been replaced and now could only be replaced by one that was a quarter of a million miles away on

Earth. I sent off a message to the company explaining my situation and waited.

By return message the company said they would be sending a replacement which should arrive in a week. It would take that long because the replacement would have to come from the manufacturer. I began wondering again, would that be in time?

I put the problem to my Emmie. Considering the size of the rocket, occupied by only one person, if the carbon dioxide scrubber failed, how long before carbon dioxide levels reached a dangerous level? The result, four days.

So, the scrubber pump needed to last at least three, or even better, four days. It was that evening that the alarm I had programmed appeared on my Emmie. The pump had overheated and shutdown the system. I had four days to find a solution. I messaged the company, they would get back to me.

Such a deadline didn't really help focus my mind and certainly did not contribute to any restful sleep. In my bunk that night with my mind churning the only solution I could think of was to have the rocket take-off and rendezvous with the station. I would wait and see what the company proposed but I had my backup plan. I turned the fan on again, the noise was comforting enough for me to fall asleep.

The next morning I still had not heard from the company, that wasn't comforting. I decided I wouldn't wait. I was going to try to take-off and rendezvous with the space station. Of course, everything would have to be done by the AI. I told the ship's Em what I wanted to do and it agreed, it would run a diagnostic and should be ready in an hour. Now, I had to confront the company and see why they were delaying.

Instead of messaging I would radio, it was afternoon and all the managers should be available.

"We've been in meetings all day Rogers, we haven't come up with anything other than what you have suggested. Of course, if you take off now without trying to repair the pump we lose any chance to meet our original goals. But we'll leave it up to you."

Dravers had said they could send me the procedure to substitute a different pump if I wanted to give it a try. It shouldn't take more than a few hours.

"All right I'm going to try to replace that pump, so send me the procedure."

I had replaced the pump just as the company had suggested but nothing was happening. The company sent me a troubleshooting checklist but after another hour, still no luck. It was getting late, I figured I had about two days of good air left. The company messaged that the replacement pump was delayed, it wouldn't get here until after my air ran out. I decided to get some rest and then have the Em take-off. Once in my bunk, after all the frustration of the day I fell asleep fast.

I woke gasping for air, something was wrong. I looked at my Emmie, I hadn't been asleep more than four hours. I sat up, breathing was still hard but better. My Emmie must have miscalculated, I checked the carbon dioxide monitor, it was borderline high and increasing. I went to put my suit on, it hadn't been recharged since the Moon walk but it should give me another hour of fresh air, more if I used it sparingly.

Making my way to the control room, I strapped into a chair and told the ship's Em to take-off and rendezvous with the station. It would be close but I thought I had enough air to make it. I heard the oxidizer pre-valves open and the glump, glump, glump as the oxidizer was pumped down the lines to the engines. Then, I heard it stop and all was quiet. My head swam as panic set in.

"What happened?" I asked the Em.

"We have a sensor in the red zone preventing the launch," said the Em through my suit radio.

"Can you override it?" I asked.

"Not possible, it is a safety measure."
I felt dizzy.
Is the air in my suit bad too?

I tried to focus.
"What sensor is it?" I asked the Em.
"It's a tilt sensor."
What in the world is a tilt sensor?

Epilogue

I was breathing rapidly, I had to calm down, I was using too much of my suit's air.

After a moment of concentration I asked, "What's a tilt sensor?"

"It's a landing pad sensor, it measures the tilt of the rocket. If it's too far out of range, a landing or take-off will be aborted."

I knew there was nothing wrong with the "tilt" of the rocket. It must be a sensor problem, another malfunction. Was I doomed?

Another moment of concentration before I could think.

What kind of sensor is it?

I used my Emmie to access the sensor manual. I discovered it was a hall effect sensor, whatever that was.

I read, 'A hall effect sensor is a solid state sensor that produces a voltage which is proportional to an applied magnetic field . . ."

I stopped, it clicked. The dust reduction grid, I knew it had been turned on after the rocket had landed, not before. Maybe?

I would have to leave the rocket and go to the porch to shut off the grid. Since I was already in my suit I simply went to the outer airlock and cycled through. It was a short walk to the porch and with the simple press of a button I de-energized the grid. A short walk back and cycling through the airlock, I was back in the control room, it had taken less than an hour, but that was a long time in my present situation.

Again strapping into a chair I told the Em to take-off and rendezvous with the station. I heard oxidizer pre-valves open and then the glump, glump, glump as the pump pushed the oxidizer toward the rocket engine. This time it didn't stop.

Some one-hundred and fifty feet below the control deck small gas cartridges released their contents causing the turbopumps to begin spinning and forcing both fuel and oxidizer into the reaction chambers of the twin engines. The rocket came to life, groaning and vibrating but not yet moving.

"Lift-off," said the Emmie.

Soon the rumble of five-hundred thousand pounds of thrust was vibrating throughout the rocket and told me I was going somewhere. The take-off wasn't nearly as stressful or loud as an Earth launch and soon I was high above the Moon's surface. I didn't know how long it would be before I rendezvoused with the station and I didn't want to know. It was going to be close and soon because of either nervous exhaustion or bad air I was calmly drifting off to sleep.

I woke up strapped in a bunk on the space station. Joan was there.

"How do you feel Jeremy?" she said.

"I'm a little tired and my head hurts," I said.

"Probably an effect of the carbon dioxide," she said.

"I made it," I said.

"You made it," she said.

"I know why the space truck wouldn't land at the job site," I said. "Same reason I almost didn't make it."

"Yeah," she said. "You'll have to put that in your report."

"Yeah, it's easy to fix, as easy as pushing a button," I said.

Moon 3D

"All civilizations become either spacefaring or extinct."

- Carl Sagan

Chapter 1

2038 A.D.

Joan Hartridge had gotten the promotion, but it wasn't in the way she would have liked. Someone had been killed and Joan was next in line (for a promotion, not to be killed).

Still, she took her job as lead foreman on the first commercial space habitat to be established on the Moon seriously. In Mare Frigoris just south of the crater Timaeus, the settlement Tima was being built by the Luna Limited company. A store of water ice had been discovered at the base of the southern wall of Timaeus and would eventually be the civic supply for the settlement.

Tima had started as a single inflatable hab transported from Earth by the Space Trucks company. Once inflated with oxygen manufactured at the Moon's south pole and nitrogen brought from Earth the hab was "rigidized" by filling a layer of the flexible wall material with a mixture of what had come to be known as "Moon cement." The cement was made from an alkali binder and the Moon's regolith, and besides rigidizing the hab, the cement also functioned as a radiation shield. It also was used around the base to anchor the hab. Fourteen crew, including Joan would live in the three-story structure for up to three months before having to rotate back to Earth. Half the crew were already on the third month of their contract.

Joan had overseen the installation of the hab and was now tasked with building the first of a series of habitats made from Moon cement and a 3D printer. The printer had arrived and some of the crew had it assembled. It was capable of autonomous movement once it was given a plan for a dwelling. The on board AI, called an Em which stood for emulated brain, handled the coordination. The only job for the crew once the printer began was keeping its tanks of cement, water, and liquid hardener filled.

MOON 3D

The two week lunar day was about to begin. In the first twenty-four hours the team would begin processing the lunar regolith stored near the Moon cement mixer. Small, AI automated bulldozer like machines, carried the material from the regolith pile over to the mixer which was under the "porch" (the aluminum framed bucky-sphere covered with a sandwich of kevlar and high atomic-weight gel which provided some protection from the ever present particle rain and radiation of the lunar "atmosphere.")

Under the porch, workers could monitor the mixer in suits that weren't as big and bulky as the normal spacesuit worn in the out-vac (*outside vacuum* of the Moon). This saved time and money as the suits were easier to put on and take off and cheaper. They could also assemble machinery brought from Earth under the protection afforded by the porch, such as the 3D printer and mixer.

The seven crew, including Joan, had the cement ready and the 3D printer in position. If all went well the printer would have the shell of the habitat printed within seventy-two hours including drying time. Air-locks and other mechanical equipment, like for heating and cooling, would be added later.

Once the mix was ready and the printer initialized, the building began. Like paste out of a tube the Moon cement began flowing. The continuous bead was four inches wide and built at a rate of about two inches per layer. The printer straddled the twenty feet wide building footprint, plus the wall thickness of three feet. The thick wall would not only provide a strong foundation but also radiation protection.

A track ran alongside the length of the building, forty feet. The nozzle moved down the nearside and then swung across the width of the building to where the end airlock would be installed and then doubled back. While building up the outside wall the printer also built the inner walls so that the building was completed in a continuous circuit.

It would work on one side until the walls were nine feet

high and then it would build the opposite side.

As the end walls built up it became apparent the opening being left was circular, as were the airlocks. Where exterior appliances such as environmental machinery needed access, one of the crew would place an access pipe into the layers before they began to harden.

After twelve hours the first crew retired and the second took over. During the third shift the walls on both sides had reached their finished height and the printer stopped. At this point the roof, which had been unfolded from its stored condition, was lifted onto the structure by a small crane seated in the back of the hauler. The six-wheeled hauler had been at the job site even before the inflatable hab had been assembled.

The roof of the structure was a very lightweight screen-like frame and would be attached with aluminum strapping to the cement walls. Once attached the printer would start up again and build the roof one layer at a time. This would take some time as the previous layer needed to be set before the next layer was started. The arch of the roof would be held up only partially by the frame but mostly by the cement, as if it were a stone arched roof.

During the third shift a new crew of seven arrived from the company's space station orbiting the Moon and exchanged places with the first crew, which took the rocket ship back to the station in preparation for returning Earth-side. The new crew foreman met with Joan.

"So how's the building going?" asked Harlan Reynolds the foreman of the new crew while both were seated in the inflatable hab's dining room.

Harlan was about five feet ten inches and had very short brown hair that had already started receding in front even though he was only in his early thirties.

"So far, so good," said Joan. "We've started the plumbing and electrical snakes as the printer continues building up the roof."

"The snakes are working?" he asked.

"Yeah, they really are," said Joan. "They can thread all the necessary wiring and tubing through the access space in the wall left by the printer. It looks like something tested on Earth will actually work out here on the Moon."

"You mean the disaster at Fontenelle?"

"Yeah, the whole project fell apart because of the reliance on only robotic labor. And the company fell apart afterward," she said.

"I was at the South Pole at the time pursuing my doctorate in lunar studies. Some were very alarmed by the failure because it might set back both robotics and lunar settlement," said Harlan.

"We've had very few problems with the robotics," said Joan. "But there have been a couple of times when the AI simply failed."

"You mean the incident with the dust tamping field and the company rocket?" he asked.

"Yeah, when the magnetic and electrical fields here at the job site which are used to attract the lunar dust and keep it out of the machinery caused the sensor malfunction on the rocket, it could have been a disaster if not for human intervention."

"Jeremy Rogers," said Harlan. "He rotated back to Earth didn't he?"

"Yeah, he told me he won't be coming back," said Joan. "But he not only saved himself but the company and our jobs. Still the companies up here push the robots on us."

"Well, hopefully we won't have anymore of that kind of excitement," said Harlan.

Joan nodded yes and they continued to discuss the project.

Harlan was on the job watching the printer add another layer to the roof when it happened.

MOON 3D

The printer rotated its print arm one hundred eighty degrees and began printing something on the surface. One of the crew immediately raced to hit the emergency stop on the main interface screen. The machine stopped.

"What happened Huey?" asked Harlan over his radio, to the printer tech.

"I don't know Harlan, it just suddenly went off program," replied Huey.

"Can you get it started again?" asked Harlan.

"Let me run some diagnostics and I'll try to restart the job," said Huey. "It shouldn't take but a few minutes."

"Okay," said Harlan, "but hurry if you can, we're trying to deliver this project under budget after what happened with the inflatable."

"Okay boss," said Huey.

Harlan called Joan and informed her of the problem, they discussed alternative strategies until Huey called.

"I'm ready Harlan," he said.

"Okay Huey, get it going," said Harlan.

Huey hit the button icon on the screen and the big machine came to life again.

Everything seemed fine for half an hour and then the same thing happened. The printer arm pivoted crazily, turned quickly and slammed into one of the crew and then the arm proceeded to repeat its printing on the Moon's surface. Again, the emergency stop was hit by one of the crew while the rest raced to the downed crew member.

"Joan, we've had an accident, get the medic ready," said Harlan over the radio.

Joan, who had not retired yet, immediately called the medic and told him to get ready for an injury.

The other crew had reached the downed man, fortunately his suit was intact and he was still conscious.

Harlan reaching the man bent over him and tried to ask him how he felt but the man didn't respond. Harlan wasn't sure, maybe the man's radio wasn't working, he would have to take the chance of moving him inside to get him treated. He motioned for two of the crew to pick the man up and carry him to the hab.

"Joan, I've got two of the men bringing Larry in, I'm going to stay out and check the printer," said Harlan.

"Understood," said Joan.

He then set his radio for a broadcast transmission, which would be heard by everyone at the job site.

"Okay," he said. "Everyone, except Huey, take a break, return to the hab, get some coffee and relax."

Harlan moved to Huey's side at the control console.

"Anything unusual Huey?" he asked.

"Diagnostics hasn't found anything," he said. "There's still some checks to make."

A minute later Huey said, "That's it, nothing in diagnostics."

"There must be something wrong," said Harlan.

Huey didn't answer, he was intently studying the screen.

Harlan noticed, "You see something Huey?"

"Nothing wrong but this is a little strange."

"What?" asked Harlan.

"Memory usage is a little high," said Huey.

"You think that's a problem?"

"I don't think it would cause the malfunction we saw but it's still unusual."

"Why?" asked Harlan.

"Because this system has been characterized exhaustively. It's not supposed to do this."

"What should we do?" asked Harlan.

"I'll have to run it by the engineers and see what they think. Let's get inside and get some of that coffee," said Huey.

Chapter 2

Larry was bruised and sore but would recover. As a precaution, he would be taken to the station where more extensive tests could be run.

"Huey found no problems except for a slight increase in memory usage which he doesn't know if its the source of the malfunction or not," said Harlan.

"Well, we can only send what we know back to the company and see if they can come up with a solution," said Joan. "Meanwhile, we've lost a whole shift and I don't think we can afford to lose another. We need to continue, but make sure we keep all personnel out of harm's way."

"Okay, I'll have a safety rope put up to create a no go zone while the printer is running. That should keep everyone safe," said Harlan.

Joan had the next shift and it didn't go well. The printer was malfunctioning more often. It took the entire shift to get the next roof layer added. No one was hurt but the project wouldn't be finished on time. Before the next shift started Joan and Harlan sat down to make a radio call to the company to inform them of the situation.

"But this printer was suppose to guarantee we would meet the deadline," said Rick Dravers, Chief Operating Officer of Lunar Limited. "If we don't finish in time we're going to have to pay penalties and we may lose customers. At the least this is going to impact our reputation and make it harder to get the investment we need to continue development."

"Understood Rick, but it's a technical problem that we can only work-around, not fix. By the way, have you heard from the printer's manufacturer?" said Joan.

"Not yet," said Dravers.

"Well, it seems to me that until they can figure out the problem and come up with a fix we'll just have to do the best we can," said Harlan.

"The problem is your best might not be good enough Harlan," said Dravers. "This could be serious guys. Anyway, good day."

Harlan looked at Joan.

"Is the company that close to failure?" asked Harlan.

"I don't know but I have heard rumors that they needed this project finished as soon as possible so as to generate some cash flow," said Joan. Supposedly they lost a big investor."

"Oh," said Harlan. "Well, the best I can do is get the next shift going and see if we can get the build finished."

But Harlan's shift didn't finish the habitat, however, it did finish the 3D printer.

"What now?" asked Harlan to Joan, as they were sitting in the break room of the inflatable.

"Well we are just eight inches short of specified thickness on the roof. It can still be finished and used, they will just have to adjust the duration of occupation for each group," said Joan.

"It will affect the heating and cooling somewhat," said Harlan. "Someone will have to recalculate the load and decide if we can keep environmental in a livable range."

"Air pressure might be affected also," said Joan.

Harlan nodded his head yes.

Instead of adding the last layers to the roof the team spent the shift taking apart the printer and beginning the installation of the airlocks. Once the airlocks were installed the team would start with the pressurization test. If successful, the interior team would be able to finish in shirtsleeve comfort.

With the airlocks installed and the seals around all the places the exterior wall was breached, the team began to prepare for pressurization. They brought up the tanks of oxygen and nitrogen. They were in the process of pressurizing the interior when Joan, who was in the inflatable hab preparing for sleep, got a call from the company.

"Joan, this is Amos, I need you to shutdown the job site."

"May I ask why sir," Joan was always deferential to the CEO of the company.

"We got bad news about the roof from the engineers. It turns out that we do need that extra eight inches of concrete for many reasons, from environmental viability to radiation shielding. They are also concerned with the pressurization of the hab," he said.

"But sir, we are pressurizing it now," she said. "Hold on sir."

Jane switched her radio to call Harlan.

"Harlan, I've got Amos on the line, stop the pressurization now, understand?"

"Understood Joan, I'm coming in," he replied.

Joan went back to the company call.

"Okay sir, I've stopped the crew. What do we do now?"

"Just hold on Joan. I'll get back to you as soon as I have the answer," he said.

Joan left her cabin and went to the break for coffee while she waited for the CEO to get back to her. Sleep was probably some time away now.

"What's happening Joan?" said Harlan, as he came in and sat down at her table.

She proceeded to tell him the details of the call.

"That's ridiculous," he said.

"What do you mean Harlan?" she asked.

"Well we can solve all those problems at once with a little Moon dust," he said.

"How?"

"Well, I figure the roof is strong enough to handle a little more regolith on it, so all we do is build up the regolith on the sides until we can create a mound over the roof. Engineers have proposed something similar for years. It was only because of the advent of 3D printers that they started talking about printing a roof instead of just scooping up one," he said.

"So more regolith would solve the environmental, radiation, and pressurization issues all at once," she said.

"Right," he said. "In fact I don't know why the engineers down there didn't suggest it to management."

"I wonder what Dravers thinks." she said.

"Was he on the call?" asked Harlan.

"No, just Amos," she said.

"That's strange, I don't think I've ever been on a call with the company without Rick Dravers being on it," he said.

"Come to think of it, I haven't either," she said.

After a pause he said, "Well, I'm going to get cleaned up. You going to stay up for awhile?"

"Yeah," she said.

"Okay, I'll see you later," he said, rising and heading for his cabin.

Joan waited another four hours before giving up. It was evening company time and she didn't expect to hear anything for at least twelve hours, so she went to bed.

When she woke up she had a message from Lunar Limited's CEO.

> Joan, we are going to put the build on pause. You are to close up the habs in such a way that they will be protected and usable for future operations. You will all be evacuated by the company rocket and eventually cycled back to Earth.

Please tell all there that I very much appreciate their efforts and I am sorry it has come to this. Also, tell them that they will receive their contracted amount even if they haven't fulfilled their service time.

Thank you,
Amos

Well that's crazy. We're not even going to discuss the situation further?

Joan and Harlan were not on the same sleep schedule but she thought she should wake him to discuss the message.

"That is crazy," said Harlan, "I wonder if Amos is getting good advice or if something else is the problem?"

"I don't know. I think we should try to contact Rick Dravers," she said.

They tried to call Dravers through the company but were told he was unavailable. But not why he was unavailable.

"Well, that was a waste, we should have known better," said Harlan.

"That's okay, I've got someone in the company that will tell me what's going on," she said.

"Hey Alice, this is Joan, can you talk?"

"Hi Joan. Yeah, I got a minute but I've got to get out of the building soon. I've been laid off and I'm clearing out my office."

"I'm here with the other job foreman, Harlan Reynolds, and we're laid off too," said Joan. "Everyone related to the Tima project is laid off. I got a message from Amos but, of course, it didn't say why. Have you heard anything more?"

"Okay," said Alice, lowering her voice, "this is what I've heard. Whether it's true or not I can't say.

"There's a fight for control of the company and it's scaring the current investors. So it's making it hard to raise money, as a matter of fact, it's impossible. So, Amos had no choice but to shutdown, otherwise our paychecks would start bouncing.

"Now, the interesting speculation is who is trying to wrest control of the company from the present management, especially Amos since he still holds the majority of the stock. The parties trying to gain control are something known as Off-World, they're based here in the states. But, and this is where it gets interesting, they may actually be getting their money from somewhere else. My sources are betting on the Chinese."

"Makes sense," said Harlan who was listening. "Ever since their economic crisis ten years ago they have fallen further and further behind other countries in cislunar space and on the Moon itself. Maybe they see this as a cheap way of getting a foothold that they haven't been able to establish on their own."

"Could be," said Joan. "But I think some of the other countries here like India and Russia might try the same thing."

"Well, whoever it is," said Alice, "they are willing to lose or win it all."

"Lose it all?" asked Joan.

"Yeah, someone said this could set off a bidding war which could bring in even bigger money," said Alice.

"Bigger than China?" asked Joan.

"Yeah," said Alice, "of course, encouraged to bid by the US government."

"Okay Alice, thanks," said Joan. "I'll let you go."

"Okay Joan, make sure you look me up when you cycle back to Earth," said Alice.

Joan sat there for a moment not speaking.

"What is it Joan?" asked Harlan.

"What she said about looking her up when I cycle back to Earth. It made me realize that we're really leaving all this behind," she said.

Chapter 3

Harlan, of course, hadn't been on the surface as long as Joan, but as he thought about it, he realized he felt the same way about leaving. After all, he had worked throughout school and all the training to come to the Moon and do what he was doing, and now he wondered if he would be back.

"Huey, how long do you think it would take us to scoop enough regolith to finish the build and pressurize it?"

"I don't know, probably a lunar day, it doesn't matter though, we haven't got that long. The rocket will be here in twenty-four hours," said Huey.

"We don't have to take this rocket home, do we?" said Harlan.

"What do you mean?" asked Huey.

"Huey, how long have you worked to get up here and do a job like this?"

"I don't know, most my life, I reckon."

"When do you think we'll get another chance if we leave now?"

"Months, no probably years, unless the company changes its mind pretty quick," said Huey.

"I think it will be years if ever," said Harlan. "The company is likely not to renew our contracts if it's taken over. And if Amos keeps control the company may be too in debt. By the time things shake out we will have to get other jobs and you know how rare jobs up here are, no matter your qualifications."

"I know," said Huey. "So what are you thinking?"

"We stay and finish the job," said Harlan. "I mean whose going to do anything about it?"

"That's like mutiny, ain't it? Couldn't we be arrested?" asked Huey.

"Mutiny? For staying and finishing the job without pay? How is that mutiny? Sounds more like dedication to me. And I think it will sound like that to the media as long as we have someone on Earth to make sure our story gets told."

"Who do we have?" asked Huey.

"Joan has someone who may take the job," said Harlan.

Harlan had approached Joan with his idea.

"I don't know Harlan, if the company wants us to vacate the premises and we don't, then it's trespassing, and *that* is breaking the law. I don't want to break the law."

"Yes, the company could charge us with trespassing and I looked it up. It's a misdemeanor crime in the state the company is incorporated in and the maximum penalty is up to twelve months in jail and a five-thousand dollar fine," he said.

"Well, that's something," said Joan.

"That's the maximum Joan, I doubt we'll get anywhere near the maximum. I would guess a warning and a small fine. After all no matter whose hands the company ends up in, I think they will be happy to be handed a finished project."

"What about the regolith cover. Is it safe?" she asked.

"It should be, but just to be sure I'm going to message a civil engineer I know and ask him to give me his opinion. He does these kinds of calculations all the time," said Harlan.

"Okay, you get the engineer's calculations and I'll think about it. Until then let's not spread this any further," she said.

"Okay, I'll have an answer in a few hours," said Harlan.

Joan was torn between Harlan's arguments for staying and finishing the job and following orders. She always followed orders and it had kept her out of plenty of trouble. But Harlan was right, the chances of getting another contract would be greatly reduced by being associated with this one if it wasn't finished successfully. No matter who was at fault, the incident would come up in any interview for a Moon job. There would be a disincentive to hire, right from the start. And if this was going to be the last chance she got then . . .

A few hours later Harlan was ready with an answer from his friend and he was waiting for Joan in the break room but she was late.

I hope she hasn't already decided, I know what a stickler she is for following rules.

After ten minutes Harlan was just about to give up when Joan walked in.

"Hi Joan, glad you could make it," said Harlan.

"Hi Harlan, well, I've been thinking quite a bit," she said.

"I know Joan, but let me tell you what I found out first," he said.

"Alright," she said.

"My buddy got back to me and he says that it shouldn't be a problem. As a matter of fact we could add more than eight inches of regolith, up to two feet before it might cause an issue.

"So what do you think?" he asked.

"It's good to get that confirmation but I already figured it would be okay, after all the moon cement is mostly regolith, so probably equivalent in weight. My real problem, believe it or not Harlan, is that I don't go against orders. I never have."

"I understand," said Harlan, "I wouldn't expect you to go against your conscience Joan. Huey, Jackson, and Marie have already expressed their intentions to stay and finish the job. So, don't feel obligated."

"That's great Harlan, they are some of the best. But I was just going to say that maybe it's time. I mean, you are probably right, this may be the last time we get to do the job we trained for most out lives. So, I'm in."

"Great Joan."

The rocket had arrived and Joan had informed the pilot over the radio that the five of them would be staying.

"Joan, I have my orders, I'm suppose to pick up all the personnel at this job site."

"I know Alan, but we've discussed this among ourselves and as the senior company representative here I take full responsibility," said Joan.

"Okay Joan, but I'm calling this in before I take off."

"Understood Alan, bye," said Joan.

Before she could get up there was a call coming in from the company.

"Let me speak to Joan," said the voice.

"This is Joan."

"Joan, what the hell is going on up there?"

"Whose this?" said Joan.

"This is Darnell Johnson. Amos had me call. We want to know what is happening. What is this about some of you refusing to leave the job site?"

"Sorry Darnell, but we want to finish the job we came here to do, that is all," said Joan.

"Joan, you had better rethink your position. This is insubordination and cause for automatic termination."

"I understand you position Darnell, but we've made up our minds," said Joan.

"Very well, consider yourselves terminated immediately, your salaries attached, and now you are in violation of the law by criminal trespass. Whether you are arrested there or upon return to Earth, you will be arrested and face charges," said Johnson.

"Understood Darnell, I'm signing off now."

Joan sat there a moment.

Funny, I'm not as scared as I thought I would be, maybe if nothing else this will give me some backbone.

"I understand you talked to Johnson," said Huey, as the five of them gathered in the break room to plan.

"Yeah, I did," said Joan turning to address them all, "and I want to tell all of you what we are in for. Darnell Johnson has made it clear that we are all immediately dismissed, and that we will be charged with criminal trespass, and that our salaries have been attached –"

"What does that mean?" asked Huey.

"It means that not only will they not pay us from here forward, but they will withhold what they already owe us," said Harlan.

"Crap," said Jackson.

"Right," said Joan. "Anybody want to change their mind."

They were all silent.

"Okay then, less get on with why we're here," she said.

The five got on with the planning. Harlan figured it wouldn't take them more than two work periods to finish, that meant thirty-six hours. That would leave them two Earth days before lunar night. After they were finished they would call for the rocket to pick them up. Four days and their careers would be over, the consequences of what they had done were becoming apparent to them all.

The regolith pour went well and finishing the pressurization of the habitat without incident. The five had brought some food and drink from the inflatable hab to celebrate. They were wearing their pressure suits and keeping the helmets close at hand just in case.

After the meal, Harlan was asked to say a few words.

He stood and said, "I'm not a public speaker but since we are all friends here, I'll try to say something. I guess we did it."

He was interrupted by applause from the others.

"I'm not going to minimize what we all are going to face on our return to Earth. I, just as you all, have never been charged with any kind of crime, no matter how minor. So our lives are about to change greatly. But even with what we are facing I have to say, for myself anyway, that I have no regrets."

There was more applause.

"I mean, I have regrets, like this is the last time I'll probably stand on the Moon, but I accomplished what I came here for, so no regrets there.

"I wonder, almost seventy years have passed since men first came here and only now do we have a place where we might actually live, here on the surface, even though we would still be relying on the Earth for much of our needs.

"Anyway, maybe, every now and then, we, that is mankind, need to finish the job we started. Maybe then, instead of christening this first house on the Moon, we would be dedicating the first city, or the first metroplex, maybe on Mars, or even on other bodies in the solar system.

"In the past seventy years, maybe more people needed to not quit, to finish the job, then who knows how far along to being a real spacefaring species humanity would be."

There was another round of applause as they all rushed up to shake his hand.

After a night's sleep, the crew began packing.

Huey ran into Harlan in the break room.

"I think I figured it out Harlan," said Huey.

"What's that?"

"Why the 3D printer went crazy. It's kind of crazy but I'd bet on it," said Huey.

"Okay, the type of AI in this machine is kind of new," he said.

"You mean emulate brain?"

"That's right, said Huey, "it's modeled on the human brain and I think they may have succeeded too well."

"Why do you say that?" asked Harlan.

"Well I looked at the pictures that I took of what it printed on the surface. It printed a name, its name," said Huey.

"It doesn't have a name just a model number," said Harlan.

"It has evolved since we turned it on," said Huey. "That's what caused the memory usage that puzzled me. It was becoming sentient in a way and its first action was to name itself."

"Well, that's great that you figured it out Huey, unfortunately it won't do us any good now," said Harlan.

"Yeah," said Huey.

Joan had informed the company that they were ready to be picked up. After lunch she got a call from Darnell Johnson.

"Joan, we can't come get you," he said.

"What do you mean Darnell? Why?"

"The rocket's already on its way to Earth," he said.

"But you are suppose to hold it for emergencies like evacuating personnel," she said.

"That's true Joan, but you and the others are not company employees anymore. We wanted to get our people on the station back here as soon as possible. You know how long it takes to cycle back to Earth from the Moon, especially those that have fulfilled their contracts," he said.

"Okay Darnell, I see what you are saying, but tell me what are we trespassers supposed to do now?"

"Well, depending on what happens with the company we can probably pick you all up after the Moon night is over but not before, we still consider it too dangerous to try a night landing with the company rocket," he said.

"So, you are telling me that we have to overnight here?" she said.

"Unless you can get another ride," he said.

"You know that a crew has never overnighted? We usually evacuate to the station. As you know since the cold makes it impossible to work out-vac," she said.

"I know that the spacesuits aren't rated for operation out in the vacuum during the two week night, but you all can stay in the inflatable. You still have some time to prepare if you start now," he said.

"Very well, goodbye," she said, "we'll see you in the morning."

"We can do it Joan," said Harlan, after Joan told him about the call.

"I'm sure we can Harlan, but it's that we have no choice, and we have no way out should we encounter an emergency during the night," she said. "And Harlan."

"Yes?" he said.

"No one has ever done it, at least not at a commercial site like this."

Chapter 4

At first the others were shocked at what the company had done. But Harlan explained that they had enough supplies and power to overnight without too much of a risk.

"We should be alright," he said, "and it will be a first for a commercial crew. It will further show that this site we're building can become a permanent home in a few years."

"Well, that's all well and good Harlan but we're still taking a chance. What happens if we have an emergency of some kind?" said Jackson.

"That's right, it could be a simple health problem that needs a medic right away, delay could be life threatening," said Marie.

"Well, I didn't say there wouldn't be challenges," said Harlan, "but in the case of a medical emergency, we've all had some training, and Joan and I even more, so we have a good chance of meeting such an occurrence."

"Harlan's right," said Joan, "so I suggest we maintain the same attitude we've had so far and look at this as a challenge. A challenge that we are all trained to meet."

The others agreed, though all were a bit apprehensive, including Harlan and Joan.

It wasn't only the fifteen days of lunar night, which wasn't as dark as an Earth night because of reflected Earth light, they faced, it was also knowing that just beyond the relatively thin cocoon of the inflatable hab there was an airless desert with temperatures over negative two-hundred degrees Fahrenheit. If the hab breached for any reason, say a micro-meteorite, would it make much difference if one died of vacuum exposure or the cold?

Jackson didn't think so, in fact, he thought he should have his head examined for agreeing to stay in the first place.

Harlan had seemed so passionate. I got caught up. It's the last time I listen to anyone, especially someone who sounds so committed. Committed is the right word though.

Jackson had agreed to check the food stores, although there probably wasn't much need since they were intended to supply fourteen people for the two week period. Jackson looked at all the freeze-dried packages and thought it would be the water supply and not the food supply that would be critical. He decided he would do something to insure enough water, at least for one.

After a long day, they had all reported back from their assigned duty and sat in the break room watching an outside camera. The Sun was almost completely gone and just like that it was the lunar night. No atmosphere meant the transition between day and night was almost instantaneous.

"Okay people, roughly fourteen Earth days and eighteen Earth hours before we will see the Sun again. I intend to get a good night's sleep," said Joan.

The five wandered off to their cabins for their first rest.

At first they all kept similar hours but after an Earth week they were drifting into different schedules. Harlan hadn't seen Jackson for two days and Marie was leaving for bed just as he was arriving but Joan was there.

"Hey Joan, how did you sleep?" he asked.

"Restless Harlan, how about you?"

"Not bad. I know Marie just left, have you seen anyone else?" he asked.

"No, not today," she said.

"Joan, I wonder if we shouldn't try to keep everyone to

some kind of schedule. I mean, would it be better for morale if we all saw each other every day?"

"I don't know Harlan, unfortunately none of us has much psychology training, but we're almost half way to daylight, so I think it's okay."

"If you say so, I just want to be sure everyone is coping well and I can't know if I don't see them."

"That's true," said Joan, "but we've got no reason to think there's a problem."

"Yet," he added.

But Jackson wasn't coping well and he wasn't sleeping well. The habitat still made noises if you listened closely. He could understand the sounds they heard as it had cooled from a daytime temperature of almost two-hundred-fifty degrees Fahrenheit to the nighttime temperature, but that should have stopped long ago. He was still hearing the pops and bumps. When would they stop?

But even worse, he had started to dread the coming of the Sun. If the racket was this bad at night, what would it be like when it warmed up? He had talked to Huey but Huey wasn't hearing it.

His hearing probably ain't as sensitive as mine.

Jackson had almost not made it into space. He had scored high on psychological tests indicating obsessive compulsive disorder but background interviews indicated no such disorder. If he struggled with it, he kept it under control when around others.

But now he was obsessed with the noise. He wondered if the 3D printed hab would have the same problem? Surely it wouldn't since it was made of regolith cement. He became convinced that if he could get there he would get some rest. He came up with a scheme.

He had learned in training that no spacesuit would function for long in the cold of the lunar night but that didn't mean they wouldn't function. He was sure he could be in the airlock of the new hab in no more than three minutes, he was pretty sure a suit would function that long without failure due to the cold. The only problem was taking enough food, and especially water, to stay alive for the rest of the lunar night. If a donkey-bot could function as long as a suit he could get the materials needed to the new hab. Then he would simply retrieve as much as he could on a few out-vacs.

Studying the donkey-bot technical data he noticed they had similar joint materials as the suits. In fact, they were made to function briefly during a lunar night although the manuals offered no guarantees.

He could load a donkey-bot and go out through the lower materials access airlock. There was no reason anyone would see him until he cycled the airlock and since he was on a different sleep-wake schedule they might not find he was gone until he was happily ensconced in the new hab. All he had to do was contact the hab's environmental and bring it online, it should take about six hours to raise the temperature to something survivable in a suit. Then another six hours to raise it to a comfortable level.

Jackson lay in his bunk thinking over his plan and listening to the alarming noises of the hab. He had to get some relief. He worried that each pop was the beginning of an integrity failure of the hab's "skin." Soon, anything was preferable to waiting for the collapse of the hab and his death in the vacuum and cold. Jackson decided it was time to act.

He went to the materials storage room and loaded up one of the donkey-bots with more than enough water and food to finish out the lunar night and be picked up. Soon, he was ready. In the airlock with the donkey-bot he cycled to the out-vac. He stepped on the surface of the Moon and begin quickly moving toward the other hab. The donkey-bot was close behind. Jackson stopped and turned to avoid a small crater, the donkey-bot didn't. The crash was severe enough to rupture the suit. For Jackson, it felt more like an intense burn than cold and it was over before he suffered.

Huey noticed the lights.

"It's got to be the 3D printed hab," he said to Harlan.

"How would the lights come on?" asked Harlan.

"Either a malfunction or someone turned them on," said Huey.

"Well, I'll find out, I'm going to wait here until I talk to everyone," said Harlan.

Harlan had talked to everyone but Jackson. A search for him had turned up the missing bot and supplies but no Jackson.

"I can't believe he would try to go to the other hab," said Joan. "Why?"

"I don't know," said Harlan. "I haven't talked to him for more than a few minutes since nightfall."

"Neither have I," said Marie.

"Yeah, he was keeping pretty much to himself," said Joan.

"I'm worried about the missing supplies," said Huey. "Especially the missing water."

"We'll have to figure out some new daily quotas," said Harlan.

"This is getting to be too much of a challenge," said Huey.

The four would have to go on water usage restrictions if they were to be sure to have enough to make it to the end of the lunar night but then they would also need to have some left over until they were picked up. And it was difficult to estimate when that would be. Harlan calculated just enough to keep them going so as to maximize the time they could remain.

There was nothing to do now but wait for rescue.

"Okay, we're close enough to lunar day," said Joan. "Let's find out who is coming to get us. I'm placing a call to Darnell."

Joan called Darnell and told him about Jackson missing and presumed dead. They were all listening in on the call.

"You're sure Joan?" said Johnson.

"He's been gone for several Earth days Johnson. He doesn't answer our calls, so I feel fairly sure he didn't survive, unless he did make it to the 3D printed hab and won't answer our calls. We'll know for sure in a few hours when the sun rises and we can leave the habitat and search," said Joan.

"Well, I hope for your sake he is in the other hab," said Johnson.

"What do you mean, for my sake?" said Joan.

"You are the senior foreman, the company will hold you responsible," said Johnson.

"I don't work for the company Johnson, remember? And I wasn't working for the company when Jackson disappeared, she said. So I'm not responsible, except in a brother's keeper sort of way," said Joan.

"Look Darnell," said Harlan, "this call is not about whose responsible for Jackson's disappearance, but if he is dead then this call is even more important."

"How's that?" said Johnson.

"So that four more people don't die," said Harlan.

Johnson was quiet.

"Okay, okay," he said. "We'll leave all that other stuff for later. Right now the question is, how do we get you out of there. I didn't tell you but the company is selling off its assets to raise money and the rocket was one of those assets."

"Well, how are you going to pick us up?" asked Harlan.

"We'll have to get Space Trucks to do it," said Johnson. "Although there is a slight problem, the company owes them money and they aren't doing anymore business with us."

Harlan had heard enough.

"Okay, I'll get us out of here," he said, "you and the company don't have to do anything. That is all, goodbye."

The others were a bit startled.
"What have you done Harlan?" asked Marie.
"We decided to take our fate in our hands two weeks ago now, and it's going to stay in our hands. Alice has a contact on Earth and I'm going to ask her to send an SOS to any company or government agency that can get us out of here. Everyone, get your stuff together, I expect it won't be long."

Harlan was right. Within an hour he had three promises of rescue, neither was from Lunar Limited. He accepted the Japanese proposal, they could get there the soonest. Now all they had to do was wait until daylight.

Joan and Harlan were in the media room waiting for the sun to break the horizon.

"I don't think there was ever a bidding war for the company," said Harlan.

"What do you mean?" asked Joan.

"I think it was mismanagement or incompetence and they were trying to keep from taking the blame."

"Wow, you mean we went through all of this to protect some reputations?" asked Joan.

"That, and also to give them enough time to close down the company and get as much money as possible out of what was left," said Harlan.

"Well, I know whose responsible for Jackson's death, if he is dead" said Joan.

Harlan nodded in agreement.

When the sun broke over the horizon the pair had the outside cameras pointed at the 3D printed hab.

"Oh no, said Joan as she saw the figure still standing with

the donkey-bot supporting it.

"He almost made it," said Harlan.

"Yeah it looks like he was turning to avoid something and the donkey-bot hit him. Must have breached his suit," she said.

"He froze instantly," said Harlan. "We'll get him and bring him back to Earth with us. That's our responsibility."

Lunar Series Glossary

Places

Fontenelle crater – 38 km diameter, 1.8 km deep located at 63.4 N, 18.9 W.

Fontenelle – South of crater Fontenelle in Mare Frigoris

Timaeus crater – 33 km diameter, 2.2 km deep located at 62.8 N, 0.55 W.

Tima – Settlement south of crater Timaeus, major setting for *Moon Hab, Moon 3D,* minor setting for *Moon Miner.*

Companies

Luna Limited – Settlement developer, building Tima.

Space Trucks – Operates LCL and LPL to/from Moon's surface.

Technology

3D Printer – A builder bot powered by an Em. Two tracks and an overhead crane like printer head deliver a slurry of Moon cement from a tooth paste-like tip to iteratively buildup structures.

EM/EMMIE – AI based on a model of the human brain. Called an Emmie when in a personal assistant device.

LCL – Lunar Cargo Lander built by Space Trucks. Three cylindrical shaped, rocket powered (both lateral and vertical thrust) bodies joined by trusses. The outside cylinders are specifically designed for personnel (see LPL) but adaptable for cargo while the center cylinder is designed for cargo only and is strapped beneath the trusses joining the outer cylinders. Twenty-five tons low lunar orbit to Moon's surface.

LPL – Lunar Personnel Lander built by Space Trucks. Two cylindrical shaped, rocket powered (both lateral and vertical thrust) bodies joined by trusses. Up to five tons of personnel and supplies from low lunar orbit to the surface.

Moon cement (Mooncrete) – Building material made from an alkali binder and regolith (mostly basalt). Used in making blocks and 3D printing slurry.

Porch – An aluminum frame bucky-sphere covered with a sandwich of kevlar and high atomic-weight gel which provides some radiation protection for out-vac activities such as vehicle maintenance and fueling.

Terms
Out-vac – A contraction of outside vacuum, a reference to the vacuum of the Moon's surface.

Acknowledgments

The book *A Pioneer's Guide To Living On the Moon* by Peter Kokh was "mined" extensively for ideas and settings and the technology for living on the Moon.

The Space Settlement Enterprise SSI50: 2019, a seminar held by the Space Studies Institute was the source of many ideas for this series and my Cislunar Series.

About The Author

D.W. Patterson lives in the USA with his beautiful wife Sarah. He studied physics and classic science fiction in college and then worked for many years as an electronic design engineer.

Now he's trying to write stories like the ones he once loved. He sometimes blogs at the website www.dwpatterson.com

Hard Science Fiction – Old School
Human Generated Content

Remembered Earth Universe Short Stories

CISLUNAR SERIES

*The **Remembered Earth Universe** covers the science and technology of the next hundred years, as mankind moves into cislunar space (defined as that space in and around the Earth-Moon system and slightly beyond), and takes tentative steps to destinations farther out.*

*It begins with an exploration of the space around the Earth and Moon in the stories that make up the **Cislunar Series**. These are the foundational stories of the **Remembered Earth Universe**.*

*Below is a list of the eight stories of the **Cislunar Series** in chronological order:*

Remembered Earth Short Stories Volume 1

US Tugs: A Short Story
When robots become as smart as humans, will we be smart enough to help them?

Prototype: A Short Story
James had made it to orbit, where he always wanted to be.

He thought the hard work was behind him, but when you are responsible for a hundred million dollar prototype, the hard work may just be ahead.

Remembered Earth Short Stories Volume 2

L1 Or Bust: A Short Story
There's a place for everyone, and everyone better know his place, at least aboard a spacecraft.

Guidance Box: A Short Story
Those that can, do, those that can't, sit it out.

But some times those that do can make a mistake. And if they don't have the integrity to face up to their mistakes, they may make the wrong decision and try to cover it up.

That could cost lives.

Remembered Earth Short Stories Volume 3

Air Brakes: A Short Story
Sometimes engineering is just engineering.

Sometimes engineering is subjugated to company politics.

And sometimes engineering is not enough when faced with criminal intent.

View Point: A Short Story
The problem with space is it takes a team.

Not a team of astronauts, but a team of technicians, a team of engineers, and a team of managers.

And different teams have different view points.

Remembered Earth Short Stories Volume 4

Space Truck: A Short Story
The rush to build a permanent Moon habitat was on.

Jose was project leader for the team that would land the equipment to make it happen.

Only there was one big problem, government. As hard as it was, regulators would make it harder.

Dark Side: A Novella
As a young lawyer, Josh was aware of the developing human

*presence in cislunar space, but only as a bystander.
He never dreamed he would ever have a role in that development.
But now he had to decide to step up and help further that
development, help build an important radio telescope on the far side
of the Moon by using the law, or stay a bystander.*

He stepped up and failed, but in failure sowed the seeds of success.

LUNAR SERIES

*Below is a list of the eight stories of the **Lunar Series** in chronological order:*

Remembered Earth Short Stories Volume 5

Moon Hab: A Short Story
Circling the Moon, alone, in a space station was easy.

It wasn't until I overnighted (remember a Moon night is two weeks of dim light) on the Moon's surface that things got difficult.

And life-threatening.

Moon 3D: A Novella
After more than fifty years man was back on the Moon. But this time he was determined to stay. And that meant building habitats with the AI-powered latest technology, such as 3D printers.

But while those who were directly involved might show dedication and courage to the job, those remaining on Earth were still more interested in money and reputation.

And that could lead to failure and even death for those on the Moon.

Remembered Earth Short Stories Volume 6

Moon Miner: A Short Story
You would think that mining on the Moon would be a dream job.

Great location, pays well, all expenses paid.

Problem was, people on the Moon were the same as on the Earth. And that could make just doing your job dangerous.

Moon Town: A Novella
Humans or AI-powered robots?

That seemed to have become the eternal question in the development of the Moon.

But as with all eternal questions, the practical answer might be, can they complement each other?

Remembered Earth Short Stories Volume 7

Moon Power: A Novella
Multiplying settlements required more, reliable power.

Two solar power farms located on either side of the string of Mare Frigoris settlements separated by a little over one-hundred-eighty degrees longitude could supply it.

An expedition to prepare one of the areas for development ran into the unexpected. The AI brought along had its own idea.

Moon Rail: A Short Story
Building a two thousand mile rail system to connect the Mare Frigoris settlements was an dangerous undertaking.

Young Graham Timothy thought he was up for the task.

But building the first few miles could be more than dangerous, it could be deadly.

Remembered Earth Short Stories Volume 8

Moon Nuke: A Novella
A steady supply of power was needed if the settlements on the Moon in Mare Frigoris were to keep growing.

But putting a nuclear reactor on the Moon was the greatest building project so far undertaken. It would take someone with more than building experience, it would take someone with courage. Especially to face off against the experts when they got it wrong.

Remembered Earth Short Stories Volume 9

Moon Plex: A Novella

Maddie Post was a good reporter who was approaching the end of a long, admirable, journalistic career.

Her last story was to be an expose on the commercial settlements built in Mare Frigoris.

She knew it would be her last story but she didn't know it might take her last breath.

Also By This Author

The Future Chron Universe

Volume numbers indicate Universe order.
Book numbers indicate Series order.

From The Earth Series

Volume 1, Book 1 – *Whatsoever You Do: A Novella*
Volume 2, Book 2 – *War Through The Pines: A Novella*
Volume 3, Book 3 – *Vigilance: A Novella*
Volume 4, Book 4 – *To Tend And Watch Over: A Novella*
Volume 5, Book 5 – *Union: A Novella*
Volume 6, Book 6 – *Circle Of Retribution: A Novella*
Volume 7, Book 7 – *Freedom From Want: A Novella*
Volume 8, Book 8 – *Break Up: A Novella*
Volume 9, Book 9 – *Kuiper Station: A Novella*
Volume 10, Book 10 – *The Cloud: A Novella*
Volume 11, Book 11 – *First Interstellar: A Short Novel*

Wormhole Series

Volume 12, Book 1 – *Mach's Metric: A Novel*
Volume 13, Book 2 – *Mach's Mission: A Novel*

Open Space Series

Volume 14, Book 1 – *Open Space: A Short Story*
Volume 15, Book 2 – *The Old World: A Short Story*
Volume 16, Book 3 – *Insurrect: A Short Story*
Volume 17, Book 4 – *Second Beam: A Short Story*
Volume 18, Book 5 – *All For One: A Short Story*
Volume 19, Book 6 – *One For All: A Short Story*
Volume 20, Book 7 – *Shotgun: A Short Story*

Volume 21, Book 8 – *Allison: A Short Story*

To The Stars Series

Volume 22, Book 1 – *First One Hundred: A Novella*
Volume 23, Book 2 – *First Dark Ages: A Novella*
Volume 24, Book 3 – *Second One Hundred: A Novella*
Volume 25, Book 4 – *Second Dark Ages: A Novella*
Volume 26, Book 5 – *Path Of The Long March: A Novella*

Wormhole Series

Volume 27, Book 3 – *Mach's Legacy: A Novel*

Robot Series

Volume 28, Book 1 – *Spin-Two: A Novel*
Volume 29, Book 2 – *Robot Planet: A Novel*
Volume 30, Book 3 – *The Lattice Of Space: A Novel*

Time Series

Volume 31, Book 1 – *Time Wars: A Novel*
Volume 32, Book 2 – *Time's End: A Novel*
Volume 33, Book 3 – *Frozen Time: A Novel*

Future Chron Collections

Volume 34 – *From The Earth #1*
Volume 35 – *From The Earth #2*
Volume 36 – *From The Earth: Complete*
Volume 37 – *To The Stars*
Volume 38 – *Mach's Metric: Complete*
Volume 39 – *Spin-Two: Complete*
Volume 40 – *Open Space: A Collection*
Volume 41 – *Time Wars: Complete*

The Remembered Earth Universe

Cislunar Series

Volume 1, Book 1 – *US Tugs: A Short Story*
Volume 2, Book 2 – *Prototype: A Short Story*
Volume 3, Book 3 – *L1 Or Bust: A Short Story*
Volume 4, Book 4 – *Guidance Box: A Short Story*
Volume 5, Book 5 – *Air Brakes: A Short Story*
Volume 6, Book 6 – *View Point: A Short Story*
Volume 7, Book 7 – *Space Truck: A Short Story*
Volume 8, Book 8 – *Dark Side: A Novella*

Lunar Series

Volume 9, Book 1 – *Moon Hab: A Short Story*
Volume 10, Book 2 – *Moon 3D: A Novella*
Volume 11, Book 3 – *Moon Miner: A Short Story*
Volume 12, Book 4 – *Moon Town: A Novella*
Volume 13, Book 5 – *Moon Power: A Novella*
Volume 14, Book 6 – *Moon Rail: A Short Story*
Volume 15, Book 7 – *Moon Nuke: A Novella*
Volume 16, Book 8 – *Moon Plex: A Novella* (In progress)

Collections

Volume 1 – *Remembered Earth Short Stories: Cislunar Series: Book 1 & 2* (Paperback only)
Volume 2 – *Remembered Earth Short Stories: Cislunar Series: Book 3 & 4* (Paperback only)
Volume 3 – *Remembered Earth Short Stories: Cislunar Series: Book 5 & 6* (Paperback only)
Volume 4 – *Remembered Earth Short Stories: Cislunar Series: Book 7 & 8* (Paperback only)

Cislunar: A Collection

Volume 5 – *Remembered Earth Short Stories: Lunar Series: Book*

1 & 2 (Paperback only)
Volume 6 – ***Remembered Earth Short Stories: Lunar Series: Book 3 & 4*** *(Paperback only)*
Volume 7 – ***Remembered Earth Short Stories: Lunar Series: Book 5 & 6*** *(Paperback only)*
Volume 8 – ***Remembered Earth Short Stories: Lunar Series: Book 7*** *(Paperback only)*
Volume 9 – ***Remembered Earth Short Stories: Lunar Series: Book 8*** *(Paperback only – In progress)*

The Manifold Earth Universe

Rocket Series

Volume 1, Book 1 – *Rocket Summer: A Short Story*
Volume 2, Book 2 – *Rocket Fall: A Short Story*
Volume 3, Book 3 – *Rocket Winter: A Novella*
Volume 4, Book 4 – *Rocket Spring: A Short Novel*

Rocket Series Collections

Volume 5 – *Rocket Season: A Collection*

The Forgotten Earth Universe

Null Infinity Series

Volume 1, Book 1 – *Null Infinity: Book 1: A Novel*
Volume 2, Book 2 – *Null Infinity: Book 2: A Novel*
Volume 3, Book 3 – *Null Infinity: Book 3: A Novel*